14.95

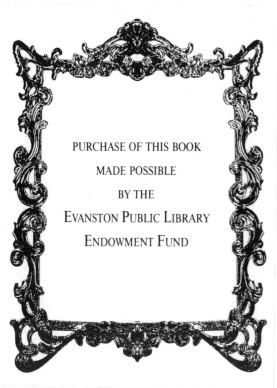

QUEEN ANNE'S
Lace

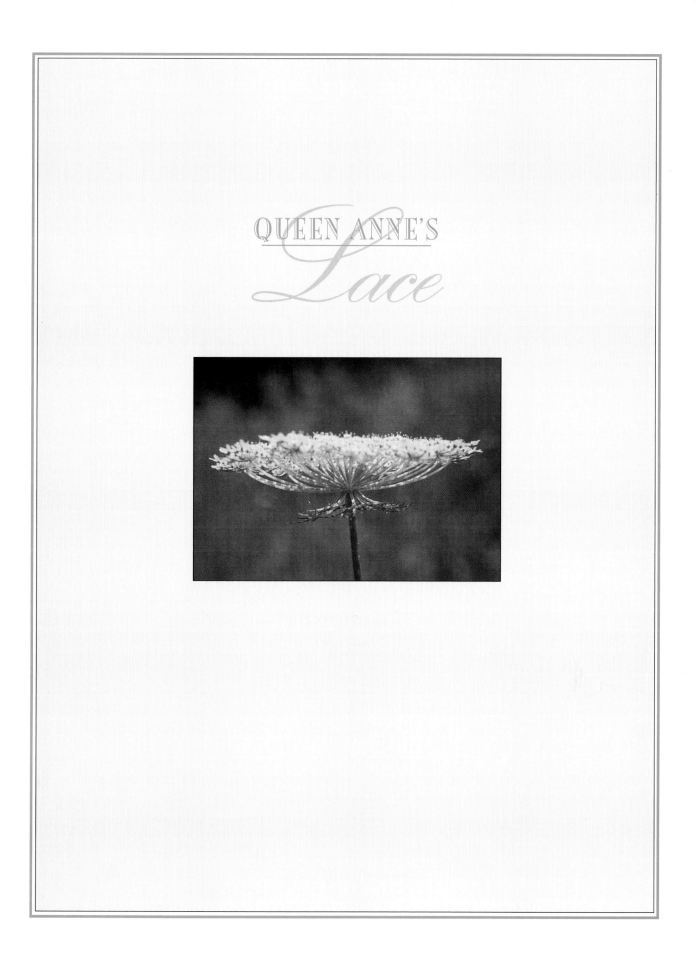

To Kathy Tucker. J. W.

Text and photographs © 1994 by Jerome Wexler.

Published in 1994 by Albert Whitman & Company,
6340 Oakton, Morton Grove, Illinois 60053-2723.
Published simultaneously in Canada
by General Publishing, Limited, Toronto.

10 9 8 7 6 5 4 3 2 1

Text and cover design: Paul Uhl, Design Associates; Chicago, IL.

Library of Congress Cataloging-in-Publication Data
Wexler, Jerome.
    Queen Anne's lace/Jerome Wexler.
        p.   cm.
    ISBN 0-8075-6710-8
    1. Queen Anne's lace—juvenile literature. [1. Queen Anne's
lace.] I. Title.
QK495.U48W44 1994   93-29621
583'.48—DC20   CIP
                                                          AC

On the back cover, the larva, or caterpillar, of a black swallowtail
butterfly climbs the stem of a Queen Anne's lace.

QUEEN ANNE'S *Lace*

Jerome Wexler

Albert Whitman & Company, Morton Grove, Illinois

How did the Queen Anne's lace get its name? No one really knows, but there's one story I especially like. In England, in the reign of Queen Anne (1702-1714), women decorated their hats and their hair with the lacy leaves of this plant. But no woman dared to wear the flower, for it was thought to be so beautiful that it should be worn only by Queen Anne herself.

With its lovely leaves, flowers, and seedheads, Queen Anne's lace is admired by a great many people throughout the world. It's gathered for bouquets and flower arrangements. Sketches and paintings have been made of it. The pattern of the flowers can be found on wallpaper, cloth, and jewelry. Many people consider the plant to be one of the most beautiful wildflowers.

Queen Anne's lace is found in Europe and many parts of Asia as well as in Canada and the northern United States. Its seeds are seldom planted, and yet it seems to grow everywhere. In fields, along streams, by roads and railroad tracks, in parks, vacant city lots, neglected yards—it just grows!

One reason the plant is successful is it can adapt to various environmental conditions. In addition to growing in good soil, it will also grow in gravelly or sandy soil as well as in soils that are a bit on the wet or dry side.

Under ideal conditions, a Queen Anne's lace may grow as tall as five or six feet and produce a tremendous number of seeds. But plant it in a small flowerpot and even though it will be less than a foot tall, flowers and seeds will still develop.

LEFT:
seedhead of
a carrot plant.
RIGHT:
seedhead of a
Queen Anne's
lace.

Surprisingly, the delicate Queen Anne's lace is similar in many ways to the carrot plant! Both belong to a large family of plants that includes many aromatic and edible herbs and vegetables: carrot, parsnip, celery, fennel, caraway, dill, parsley, coriander, and cumin.

The Latin name of the family is *Apiaceae* (ay pee AY shuh). Now, in almost every large family (human, animal, or plant), there are usually one or more unpopular members. The *Apiaceae* family contains several. Two, the water hemlock and the poison hemlock, are considered to be two of the most poisonous plants in the United States. (Never put any part of any wild plant in your mouth, for you may end up violently sick or even dead!)

When a Queen Anne's lace and a carrot plant are placed side by side, you can see that their flowers, leaves, seedheads, and roots are very similar.

The flower of a carrot plant.

LEFT: leaf of a carrot plant. RIGHT: leaf of a Queen Anne's lace.

Below is the flower of a Queen Anne's lace.

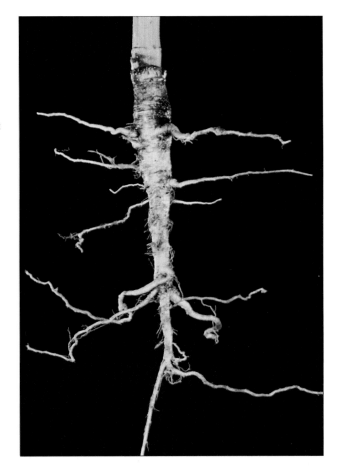

The taproot of a Queen Anne's lace after its first growing season.

Almost all members of the *Apiaceae* family are *biennials*.

A biennial is a plant that normally lives two years, producing its

flowers and seeds in the second year and then dying.

Both plants, the Queen Anne's lace and the carrot, produce

two kinds of roots: *fibrous* roots (soft, hairlike roots that grow

LEFT: fibrous roots surrounding the taproot of a Queen Anne's lace after its second season. RIGHT: the taproot of a carrot plant after its first season.

in all directions) and *taproots* (large, thick, stiff roots that normally grow straight down). Usually a plant has just one taproot, but there may be several. When we eat a carrot, we are eating its taproot. (Carrots should be eaten during their first growing season, for by the end of the second season, they are often tough and woody.)

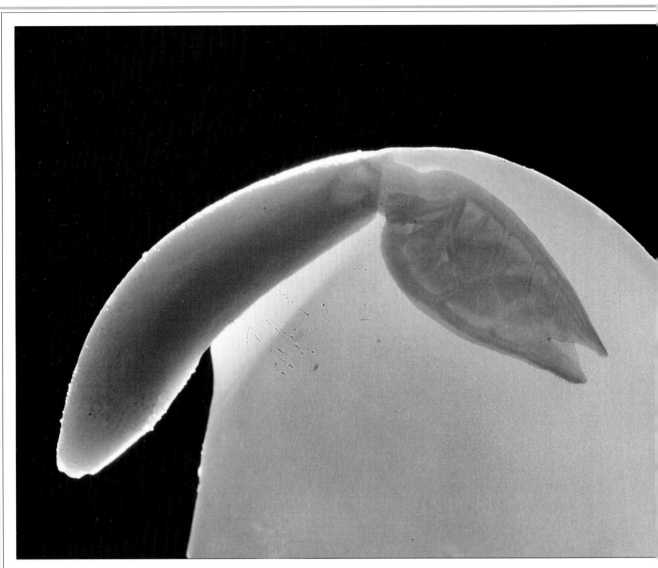

ABOVE: cotyledon seed leaves within a lima bean.
RIGHT: cotyledon leaves and the first true leaf of a Queen Anne's lace.

The seeds of the Queen Anne's lace plant usually *germinate,*
or begin to grow, in springtime, although some may not sprout
until early summer. The plant's first leaves are long and thin and
are called *cotyledon* (kaht uhl EED uhn) *leaves* or *seed leaves.* These
leaves are already formed, in miniature, within all seeds. To see
cotyledon leaves within a seed, soak a large dried seed, such as a
lima bean, in water overnight. In the morning, remove its "skin"
and separate the two halves. See the tiny leaves?

After the seed germinates, it grows rapidly and produces its
first true leaves. These look quite different from the seed leaves.
The leaves soon become larger, with more divisions.

In its first year, a Queen Anne's lace produces a *rosette*, a circular cluster of leaves that grows close to the ground. The flowers are born in the second year, on long stems that usually grow from an *axil,* a point where a leaf comes out of the main stem.

Occasionally a Queen Anne's lace is so vigorous that a flower stem will grow out of a flower!

The flower is supported by a whorl of *bracts* three to four inches in diameter. (Bracts are special leaflike parts at the base of a flower.) But the flowers grow so large (some can be six inches in diameter) that the bracts are quickly hidden from view.

Removing the flower exposes the beautiful and lacy bracts.

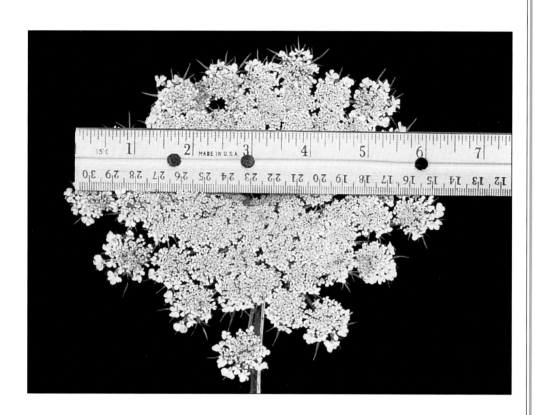

    As the flower begins to expand, it is usually tinted a greenish-white. At maturity, it turns white.

Some flowers are spherical in shape, some are concave, and some have a more or less flat top.

What we have been calling a flower is really many clusters
of small flowers called *florets*. Each cluster of florets sits at the end
of a short, thin stem called a *rib*. The ribs, looking very much like the
ribs of an umbrella, radiate from a point just above the bracts.
All the florets together are called the *flowerhead.*

Each floret has five petals, and all of the petals are the same
size, except for the outermost petals on the outermost florets. These
are oversized by two to four times. No one knows why! Do these
big petals help the plant in some way?

Each flowerhead usually has a very dark, almost black, single floret at its center. However, occasionally one can find flowerheads that have a white center floret or a small cluster of colored florets varying from light pink to deep red or purple.

ABOVE:
stamens on
a floret. (The
stigmas have
fallen off
this floret.)

BELOW: the two
stigmas of the
pistil, with
styles leading
into the ovary.

ach floret has both male and female parts. The male, or pollen-producing part, is called a *stamen*. The female, or seed-producing part, is called a *pistil*.

The uppermost part of the stamen is the *anther*. It produces pollen, which contains sperm cells. The anther sits on a threadlike stalk called a *filament*. There are several stamens on each floret.

In the very center of each floret is the pistil. Its uppermost part is called the *stigma*. At the bottom is the ovary, which contains unfertilized egg cells. The ovary is connected to the stigma by a stem called a *style*.

When an insect walks across the flowerhead, it picks up pollen from the anther of one floret and deposits it onto the stigma of another floret (on the same flowerhead or on another one). This process is called *pollination*. Once on the stigma, the pollen grain sends a tiny tube down the style into the ovary. The sperm cell goes down the tube and unites in the ovary with an unfertilized egg cell. Now the egg cell is fertilized, and the seed begins to grow.

The ovary of a Queen Anne's lace has two egg cells. Two sperm cells can enter it, and two seeds can develop.

After the petals fall, the entire flowerhead partially closes, forming a "cup," which is sometimes called a "bird's nest." Inside, protected by the long, stiff ribs, the seeds continue to grow.

Each floret can produce two oval seeds each about an eighth of an inch long, or about the size of the head of a pin. Because the seeds grow in such close contact with each other, they appear to be just one.

As the seeds mature, each flowerhead gradually turns brown and closes more tightly. The fully mature seeds are now trapped within what is now called the *seedhead.*

Nature is full of surprises. By late fall or early winter, the entire Queen Anne's lace plant is stiff, brown, dried out, and dead—yet the seedheads move! They open and close, and will continue to do so for years!

Why and how can a dead plant move? For what purpose?

How can a dead plant know when to open or when to close?

Two Queen
Anne's lace
seeds, still on
their stem,
next to the
head of a pin.
The seeds
are covered
with barbs.

Here is the answer. Each seedhead produces a great many
seeds. If all fell to the foot of the mother plant, after germinating they
would compete with each other for food, water, and light. None
of them would do well. It would be better for the individual plants
and the entire species if the seeds were scattered. To help in scatter-
ing, the seeds of a Queen Anne's lace have evolved barbs, or tiny
hooks. When an animal brushes against an open seedhead, the barbs

hook onto the animal's fur, and the seeds are carried off to fall back to earth at some new spot. (You can check this for yourself. Brush a sock against an open seedhead. See how the seed sticks to it?)

When an animal's fur is wet, it is too slippery for a barb to "hook" a ride. On a rainy day, if an animal brushes against a seedhead, a few seeds will simply be bumped off to land at the foot of the mother plant.

Moisture, then, is the key. The movement of a seedhead depends on the humidity, or moisture, in the air. When the humidity is high, the way it is on a rainy day, the seedheads react by closing. When the humidity is low, the way it is on a dry, sunny day, the seedheads open.

In late fall or winter, find the open seedhead of a Queen Anne's lace and bring it home. Place the head in a bowl of water for three or four minutes. It will close in a minute or two. Shake off the excess water, and then stick the stem in a small ball of clay to hold it upright. Watch the seedhead slowly open as it dries. This may take as long as a day.

You can repeat this experiment as often as you wish. Each time, the seedhead will close when wet and open when dry.

Want to have some fun with your friends? Make a bet that you can make a dead object move without touching it!

And you thought a Queen Anne's lace was just another pretty flower!